This book is dedicated to my hero: my Dad, Thomas James McGuire, who passed away peacefully on my birthday, May 1, 2019.

www.mascotbooks.com

Santa Fe Tom

For more information, please contact:
Mascot Books
620 Herndon Parkway, Suite 320
Herndon, VA 20170
info@mascotbooks.com

Library of Congress Control Number: 2019918388

CPSIA Code: PRT0220A
ISBN-13: 978-1-64543-269-2

Printed in the United States

SANTA FE

TOM

Rachel Bate

Illustrated by Rebecca Jacob

It was a bright sunny morning in New Mexico, at the very end of May. Desert Box Turtle Tom gave a small yawn to welcome the day.

With his hind legs, he carefully crept out of his hibernation home. His cute little shell looked like a very muddy dome.

All of a sudden, he heard a loud cry. He blinked and he blinked with his sleepy red eyes.

"It's time to get ready! The party is soon! We all must practice a surprise birthday tune!"

Now, Tom was a shy turtle who hardly ever spoke. So, Ray Roadrunner looked at him curiously and gave Tom's shell a poke.

"Come on, hurry up, and stop messing around! It's time to get moving, and drive to Critter Town!"

Quincy Quail, Molly Mockingbird, and Paul Prairie Dog had just arrived. They were waiting to go and practice for the big birthday surprise.

"Hurry Tom and Ray, we have to get ready! Hold on to the wagon, and everyone keep steady!"

They all jumped in and held on extremely tight. Crossing the desert brush, oh my, what a sight!

They arrived at the practice venue, and the critters gathered inside. They joined in the shade where they could practice safely and hide.

"Alright, are you all ready to rehearse the birthday song? Everyone must participate, and even Tom must sing along!"

Shy Tom was so nervous and started turning red. The thought of singing made him feel sick with dread.

He crawled in his shell, hiding as best as he was able, while the other critters started to practice at the decorated table.

"Tom," his friends cried, "please get out of your safe little shell. We know if you try, you'll do very well!"

Slowly, oh so slowly, Tom quietly crept out, as he listened to the tune that the others began to shout.

Tom started to sing with all his quiet strength, and suddenly there was silence, for a period of length.

The critters were ecstatic and in quiet awe, hearing their shy friend Tom whose beautiful voice none could recall!

"Tom, you must audition for the Santa Fe Critter Opera House!" exclaimed Jody the jumping kangaroo mouse.

"Your voice is natural and so very new. I predict the audition crowd will fall in love with you, too!"

Then Molly Mockingbird exclaimed, "Wait, hold the phone! Did everyone forget? We have a surprise birthday song, on a deadline we set!"

Off the critters went, over the desert brush. They traveled in haste, they were in such a rush!

Finally, the critters reached their destination. They spotted birthday girl Tierra in the garden, her main fixation.

The critters created three neat rows and began to sing, as Ray Roadrunner led the chorus with his long feathery wing.

When they all stopped singing, Tom continued the song. Tierra, shocked at the shy little turtle, in disbelief listened on!

"Thank you! Oh, thank you!" Tierra said with a sigh. "This is the best surprise ever," and wiped a tear from her eye.

Then there was a yell from Jody, the joyful mouse, "Tierra, we must now rush to the Santa Fe Critter Opera House!

Tom is auditioning for a tenor singing part, and we'll all be late if we don't get a start."

They headed out on the highway towards Santa Fe. What a beautiful sunset they saw on the way!

Poor shy Tom started to tremble — he was so filled with fright. He began to worry about performing this very same night.

In Tom's ear, Tierra whispered, "Be brave, little friend! Don't stop singing until the very end!"

Can I really do this? Tom meekly thought. He took three deep breaths as his shy nerves he fought.

All of a sudden, he heard a giant roar, "Bravo, bravo! Can we please have more?"

Slowly, oh so slowly, his confidence grew. His tenor voice was wonderful and would be hard to subdue!

At the end of his song there was a standing ovation. His humble heart was full of successful gratification.

I did it, I did it! he silently said, as his face slowly turned to normal, from a deep dark red.

Tom was greeted at the end of the night, and was told he had the lead in the opera, to everyone's delight.

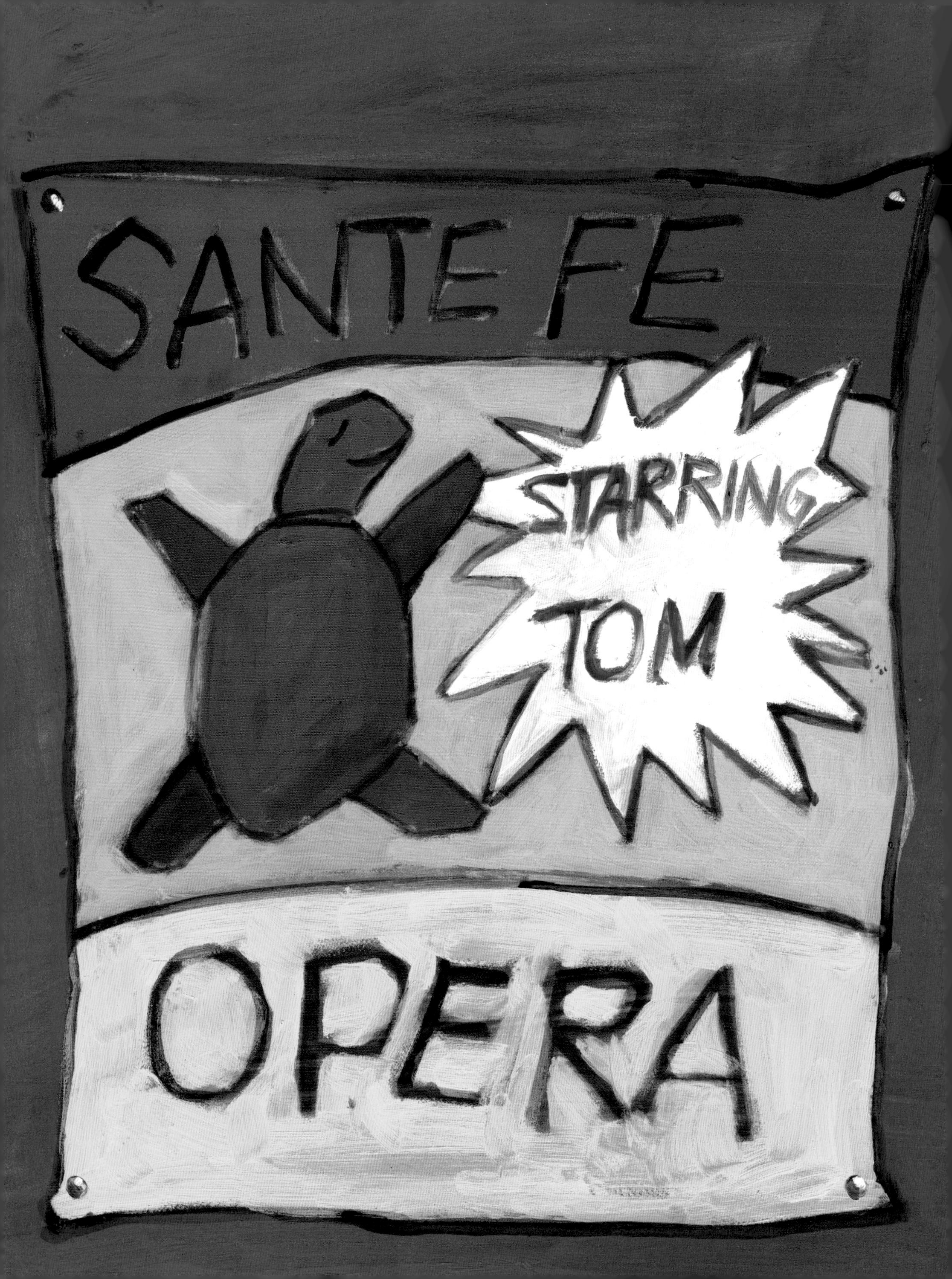
SANTE FE
STARRING TOM
OPERA

To this day, the once-shy turtle is known as "Santa Fe Tom," the talented tenor, who now sings with aplomb.

Tom's stardom did not at all go to his head, for he stayed the way he always was, a kind humble turtle, enough said.

Interesting Desert Box Turtle Facts

- Desert box turtles can be found in the southwestern United States, including west Texas, New Mexico, and Arizona. They can also be found in Northern Mexico.

- The habitats of desert box turtles include grasslands, prairies, and regions that are arid and semi-arid. Desert box turtles need soil that is easy to dig for nesting and hibernating.

- The average length of a box turtle is 35 cm. It has a hinged shell that can completely close to protect itself.

- The male desert box turtle has red eyes and the female has brown eyes.

- A desert box turtle eats a diet mostly of insects, but it will also eat plants and berries.

- Box turtles are not adults until they are ten years old. Some can live for as long as fifty years or more.

Reference: www.boxturtles.com

*This is a picture of **Tomi,** a female Desert Box Turtle, who visits the author's back patio in the morning and early evening every summer. Photograph courtesy of the author's niece, Madeline Jacob.*

About the Author

Rachel McGuire Bate has written two children's books, *Desert Bliss*, a finalist in the Indie Excellence Book Awards and Best Book Awards, and *Turquoise Tail*. Her third book, *Santa Fe Tom,* once again features critters of the New Mexico desert, a passion of her love of nature and her home. Every summer a wild desert box turtle visits her backyard, which gave her the inspiration to write *Santa Fe Tom*. As a first-grade teacher, she also wrote this story for all children to help them face their fears and overcome shyness.

About the Illustrator

Rebecca McGuire Jacob illustrated the artwork for *Desert Bliss, Turquoise Tail,* and *Santa Fe Tom.* Rebecca, an artist, works out of her art studio in Pennsylvania and visits New Mexico frequently to visit her sister, the author, and for inspiration for future artwork.